An Amish Quilt to Warm the Heart

By
Ruth Bawell

AF430925

Copyright © 2020 by Ruth Bawell

All rights reserved.
No part of this book may be
reproduced, stored in a retrieval
system, or transmitted in any form, or
by any means, electronic, mechanical,
photocopying, recording or otherwise,
without prior permission of the author
or publisher.

Printed in the United States of America

Table of Contents

Unsolicited Testimonials

By **Phyllis**

⭐⭐⭐⭐⭐ **Love Ruth!**

I love Ruth's books! Her mysteries are the best!

⭐⭐⭐⭐⭐ **Love This Author**

Ruth Bawell is very creative and a great writer! All her books have left me unable to stop reading till the ending! There were a few Amish fact mistakes, like unmarried man having a beard, but the plot was so good I overlooked that!

By **Steve M**

⭐⭐⭐⭐⭐ **I love romance stories** August 5, 2017
I love romance stories... well written with her usual twists to the story still enjoyed them very much Once I start I can't put it down.

By **Bones**

⭐⭐⭐⭐⭐ **Amish County Stories**
I love all the Amish County stories! Each one brings so much excitement! Ruth Bawell is also a wonderful writer!

By **Kindle Customer**

⭐⭐⭐⭐⭐ **Good clean writing.**
The Amish stories of Ruth Bawell are authentic, faith-filled writings. They are short, more the length of novellas or longer short stories. Always clean, always uplifting.

FREE GIFT

Just to say thanks for checking our works we like to gift you

Our Exclusive Never Before Released Books

100% FREE!

Please GO TO

`http://cleanromancepublishing.com/gift`

And get your FREE gift

Thanks for being such a wonderful client.

Chapter One

"Peter!" Bethany called to her three-year-old son who was playing in the snow, "come inside now, it's supper time!"

"Coming, *Mamm*!" Peter replied, obediently moving away from the group of children and coming towards her.

"*Mijn kinderen*!" Bethany addressed Peter's playmates. "You can come too, if you like!"

But the children had scattered and were running towards their respective houses.

Bethany sighed as she took Peter's gloved hand in hers. She would have been glad of the company and a house filled with children's voices.

Peter looked up at her, and she swallowed her pain and forced a smile onto her face.

"Come on little one," she said, swinging him up into her arms, "there's beef stew for supper and soft warm bread, right out of the oven, with homemade butter."

As she sat across from Peter at the kitchen table, gazing at his face aglow in the lamplight, she kept up a constant flow of conversation with her little son. Filling the space with chatter helped her forget the void in both their lives—a void that made winter seem bleaker than ever. A well of sorrow had submerged her when she had tragically lost her husband, Ezekiel, a year after Peter was born. How grateful she was that Peter didn't realize that Ezekiel was gone, never to return.

After she had put Peter to bed, she stood by the window looking at the snow falling outside. A stray tear found its way down her lovely face. She couldn't escape the fact anymore. After the last harvest, which was less than satisfactory, she knew that she might have to sell the farm. Ezekiel had been passionate about it, and it had thrived under his care. But she had been unable to yield the same results, despite taking on extra farmhands and spending time out in the fields.

She was still thinking about the farm the next day, when she was driving her buggy with Peter sitting by her. She was so engrossed in her thoughts, she failed to see the man walking briskly down the side of the street. Her grip on the horse's reins had slackened as her spirits sagged, and the buggy veered off to the side.

"Hey! What do you think you're doing?" a voice shouted out.

Jerked into consciousness, Beth gasped, tugging at the horse and bringing the buggy to a standstill.

"I'm so sorry!" she cried. She jumped off the buggy and stared in dismay at the young man she had collided with and inadvertently knocked to the ground. "I didn't see you!"

"Clearly," the young man retorted.

"I really do apologize," Beth said, contrite and concerned. "Are you alright?"

The young man attempted to rise to his feet and winced in pain.

"I may have twisted my ankle when I fell, but I need to check," he replied coldly. "Do the residents of Hazel Grove Village always give their horses free rein to go where they want, thus endangering the lives of stray passersby?"

Beth dropped to her knees beside the young man. "Let me take a look at your leg," she said, ignoring his aggrieved tones. He was clearly still shook up from being run down.

"Do you have any medical training?" the man asked irritably.

Beth flushed. "No, but I grew up on a farm and have dealt with a few accidents." She blanched visibly as she saw blood on the young man's trouser leg. "Oh dear, I am truly sorry for what I've done."

"I'd best find my way to a doctor," the young man murmured.

Beth squirmed inwardly. "I'm sorry mister…"

"Beiler. Solomon Beiler," the young man replied, not looking up from his leg. He attempted to staunch the flow of blood with a handkerchief that he extracted from his coat pocket.

"As you might be aware, the closest doctor is a thirty-minute buggy ride away," Beth remarked.

"No," Solomon replied coldly. "I'm not aware. I'm new to this village. And had I known that there were careless drivers around and no doctor for miles, I might not have indulged my passion for long walks so hastily."

"Please, Mister Beiler," Beth murmured, getting to her feet, "If you would allow me to drive you back to my farm, which isn't far away, I could tend to your wound."

"*Mamm*!" Peter called suddenly.

"Oh, Peter!" Beth exclaimed, "I almost forgot you were there!"

Solomon Beiler gave her a disapproving look. "Miss…"

"Bethany. Beth. Fischer," Beth said.

"Miss Beth, forgive me if I'm wrong, but you seem distracted—first knocking me down and now forgetting you have a small child in your buggy," Solomon observed.

Beth flushed, wincing at the barb. "Come with me," she said. "I will tend to your wound without further delay."

As the buggy drew up outside Beth's farm cottage, she turned to Solomon.

"Should I help you down?" she asked.

"I can help myself, thank you," Solomon replied.

Beth climbed down with Peter in her arms and led Solomon inside the house. A farmhand came to take the horse and buggy to the stables.

Once inside, Beth set to work with antiseptic lotion and bandages, making sure the wound was cleaned and expertly bound.

"Thank you," Solomon murmured grudgingly.

"You're welcome," Beth replied. "Please, do keep seated while I fetch you a cup of cocoa."

"I expect your husband is out at work on the farm," Solomon observed some minutes later, as he took a sip of his cocoa.

Beth turned away and shook her head. "Sadly, no," she replied softly. "He passed away… two years ago."

Solomon set his mug down and turned to Beth with his eyes very wide. Suddenly, he felt embarrassed for reacting in such an irritated way. The woman had been nothing but kind to him, after running him over.

"I am so sorry," he declared. "And I am very sorry for being annoyed with you. I overreacted, and was a bit confused. "

"You weren't to know," Beth replied hastily. "And I did do something wrong by not paying attention while I was driving. It's just that things haven't been the same…" Her voice trailed off as she realized she was saying more than she needed to. "I can drop you home," she said instead.

"I can walk," Solomon replied. "I really enjoy walking, you know."

"Perhaps not with your injury," Beth replied. "Please let me help you get home. It's the least I can do after knocking you down."

***

"How do you manage the farm all by yourself?" Solomon asked as Beth drove him to his house.

"I have farmhands," Beth replied. "But despite that, it's been a hard few years."

"I suppose it would be," Solomon remarked sympathetically.

"So, you're new to our village?" Beth asked, swiftly changing the subject.

"Yes, I've just moved to Lancaster County from Ohio," Solomon answered. "I bought a house, but now I'm looking to invest in some land for a farm."

"I see," Beth murmured.

"You wouldn't happen to know of any land going in these parts, would you?" Solomon asked.

"I'll be sure to let you know if I do," Beth replied, as she expertly maneuvered the buggy into the lane leading to Solomon's house.

Chapter Two

"Can *Onkel* Sol come to play with me tomorrow?" Peter asked hopefully.

Beth looked up from the quilt she was working on by the fire and shook her head.

"We can't trouble him, Peter," she replied. "But I'm sure that he will play with you if he comes to visit."

"Is he coming?" Peter asked eagerly.

"I don't know, my son," Beth answered with a smile, her head bowed over her work. Peter didn't know it, but she had been wondering the same thing herself. Solomon had taken to coming around from time to time, and he had become quite fond of Peter already.

"You say your farm isn't doing well?" Solomon had asked when they met last.

Beth had nodded and sighed. "Perhaps I'm not as good at running a farm as my Ezekiel was," she said.

"Or maybe you just need more help and advice," Solomon remarked. "Both of which I would be happy to offer." He gave her a self-deprecatory smile and shrugged. "I just feel like I need to make up for the way I behaved when you

knocked me down entirely by accident," he *declared.*

"I feel mortified just thinking about how I went off the road and did that," she replied. *"And you shouldn't feel like you have to make up for anything. I made a mistake and you reacted. I'm just glad you weren't seriously hurt and that you're fine now."*

"Well, if you need any help, please don't hesitate to ask," Solomon said.

"You look sad, *Mamm*," Peter remarked, drawing her attention back to the room.

Beth laid her quilt aside and lifted her son onto her knee.

"Now how can I look sad when you make me so happy?" she replied, giving him a hug.

The little boy hugged her and smiled, and she let her worries calm as she held her sweet boy in her arms.

A knock on her door brought Beth to her feet.

"*Onkel* Sol!" Peter purred hopefully. Beth made her way to the door, thinking it was far too late for Solomon to come for a visit.

"Rhoda!" she exclaimed, opening the door to her neighbor. "What brings you here?"

She opened the door wide and set some water to heat on the stove. After a few moments of pleasant chat, Rhoda got to the point of her visit.

"You know we all love you here in Hazel Grove, don't you Beth?" Rhoda said, taking a seat and sipping the cocoa that Beth placed in her hand.

"Of course," Beth replied, looking mystified. "And you know how much I love you all."

"I don't want to do this, but I have to, Beth," Rhoda continued.

"You're making me worried now, Rhoda," Beth murmured, leaning forward and taking her friend's hand.

"Look, Beth," Rhoda went on, "we all want the best for you and we really want to help you. But remember the money I lent you…"

"Oh," Beth whispered, dropping Rhoda's hand and leaning back with a troubled sigh. "I requested you to please give me just a couple more months, Rhoda," she said. "And I have made the same request to the others I borrowed from as well."

"I need the money, Beth," Rhoda declared. "I can't wait much longer, I'm afraid. And the others who lent to you, well, they sent me to speak on their behalf. You see, the year was not kind to any of us."

"So you all got together and discussed this matter?" Beth asked, embarrassed.

"We had to," Rhoda answered. "We were trying to find a way to give you more time, but we realized we couldn't. Beth, I hope you understand that I'm not happy doing this. I know what a struggle it is for you, bringing up a child all by yourself and running the farm alone. But you've given it a go and it's just not working, is it? Personally, I don't think you were cut out for the job. I admire your persistence, but maybe you should give yourself a break, my dear, and let it go. I'm sure you'll find a good buyer who will give you enough to pay your debts while leaving you enough to live on."

Beth's face crumpled up and she began to cry, despite her best efforts to keep her emotions under control.

"Oh, dear," Rhoda said, as Peter came running to his mother and threw his arms around her neck, "I am so sorry I had to have this conversation with you."

"I know you are," Beth said, in between sobs. "But this place... this farm... it's all I have left of..."

"I understand," Rhoda replied. "And I know how much you miss him, but Beth, this may be for the best. Maybe this is a way for you to move on."

"Rhoda, you'll never know how many times I have considered selling and moving," Beth replied. "I have never talked about it—just let the thoughts come and go. Sometimes they have kept me up at night because selling the farm may be the only option I have."

"Well," Rhoda said, trying to be helpful, "you do make lovely quilts. Maybe you could find a way to sell them?"

"Thank you for that," Beth said, "but they would not be enough to pay my debts."

She dried her eyes and continued, "But please tell everyone that they don't need to worry. I will do whatever it takes to make sure you all are paid back before too long. And thank you, Rhoda, for being so patient and lending me money to tide me over through the toughest times."

"That's what friends are for, Beth," Rhoda reassured her.

***

The next day, Beth was making tea when she heard the sound of a buggy outside her house.

"I'm sorry to interrupt you in the middle of the day," Solomon said, coming up the porch steps.

"Oh, there's not much one can do in the snow," Beth replied, "though I am using the time to study about new farming techniques for a better yield."

"Oh?" Solomon murmured, as he followed Beth into the cottage and took a seat.

"Yes," Beth replied, sitting down opposite him. She had decided to give the farm one last go, and would use the winter to learn all she could.

"*Onkel* Sol!" Peter whooped, racing out of the adjoining room and throwing himself at their visitor.

"Hello, Petey!" Solomon grinned, picking Peter off the ground and swinging him up into the air. Peter yelled with glee, and for a while Beth just sat there staring at them, soaking in the sound of happy voices.

"I'm sorry," Solomon apologized, setting Peter down and preparing to resume his conversation with Beth. "You were saying you're learning about farming."

"Please don't apologize," Beth said hastily. "This is what Peter misses… and needs."

"Do it again!" Peter demanded, holding his arms out to Solomon.

"I have a better idea," Solomon said. "If you could give me one moment to talk to your *Mamm*, I'll take you out to play in the snow."

As Peter nodded, grinning broadly, Solomon looked at Beth hesitantly.

"You look serious," Beth remarked.

"Actually, I am," Solomon replied. "I just came over to make you an offer for your property, so that you don't have to study new farming techniques."

Beth wrung her hands, unable to say anything.

"So someone in the village must have prompted you to come and make the offer," she said eventually.

"I don't understand what you mean," Solomon answered, looking mystified. "You know I've been looking for some land, and I just thought it might be of some help to you if I…" He stopped, bit his lip and stood up.

"I'm sorry," he said. "I realize how important your farm is to you. Obviously, you wouldn't want to sell it."

"Please give me a day or two," Beth said. "I am afraid that I do have to sell it. To be honest, I am in debt to a few people in our village. They have been nothing but understanding, giving me a lot of time to repay them, but their own need is making them impatient." She paused and took a deep breath. "So the land is yours, if I must let it go. But please give me a day or two as I explore one more option."

"Which is?" Solomon asked.

"To sell my quilts," Beth replied with a small shrug.

"Could I take a look at them?" Solomon asked.

Beth pointed to a table behind him.

"Oh my!" Solomon exclaimed, gaping at the array of exquisitely made quilts displayed there. "They're exceptional!"

He picked them up one by one, examining the craftsmanship. Each one was clearly handmade, with fine stitching and intricate detail.

"I'm certain that any large store would be happy to buy them," he declared.

"Oh," Beth said. "I was thinking more about going house to house right here in the village."

Solomon's eyes were sympathetic as he spoke. "Beth, you don't have to do that. It would take too much time away from Peter, wouldn't it?"

Beth looked up at him uncertainly. "I suppose I will have to take him with me when I go out selling them," she declared. "Or… I could sell this property and move elsewhere… and start over."

"Don't worry, Beth," Solomon hastily reassured her. "We'll think of something. In the meantime, I would be glad to buy, for whatever price you name, all those quilts on that table, and any more you may have."

"You don't have to, Solomon," Beth replied. Her expression seemed to close a bit, and she took a half-step back as she turned to pick up the empty teacups. "And you don't have to feel like you need to make amends for justifiably being upset with me for knocking you down."

Chapter Three

Solomon left Beth's cottage feeling more than a little overwhelmed. He hadn't meant to offer to buy all the quilts, and when he made the offer and saw Beth's face, he knew he had crossed a line, and one that he needed to examine carefully. He had no idea why, but ever since he had encountered her on the side of the street, looking up into her distraught face, he had felt a strange mixture of emotions that he hadn't yet made sense of. What's more, ever since he had heard that she was alone in the world, but for little Peter, he'd felt the need to protect her.

Solomon chastised himself as he recalled Beth's reaction to his offer to buy all her quilts…

"You're doing it to be kind, Solomon," Beth said, *"and though I really do appreciate it, I can't let you do that. It simply isn't right."*

"Well, may I at least buy one?" Solomon asked.

"Of course," Beth replied. *"And Solomon, thank you for giving me a little extra time."*

"Take all the time you need," Solomon said, choosing a quilt.

Beth smiled a slow, sad smile. "Now if only I had all the time I needed," she said, *"but the fact is, I don't. I can't have my way in this matter. I realize that."*

"I will come around tomorrow with the payment for this beautiful quilt," Solomon said as he left.

He drove his buggy out onto the street and kept going, spurred on by a burning need to make a trip to town.

***

Meanwhile, Beth stared gloomily out of the window. That Solomon would even think of buying every one of her quilts in order to help her pay her debt was a gesture that disturbed her rather than set her mind at ease. She was aware of her predicament and dire need at that moment, but she wasn't about to let anybody pity her to the extent that they would buy all her quilts when they obviously didn't need them.

He had been so kind, had Solomon. Now, her surge of emotions past, she chastised herself a bit for being so defensive. Beth smiled as she remembered how he had kept his word to Peter and taken him outside to play. He had returned to pick out the quilt he wanted, and then left, looking embarrassed at having made an offer to buy them all.

But maybe they had made it all okay during their goodbye.

"I didn't mean any disrespect," Solomon *had said.*

"I know," Beth *replied. "You are being kinder than you should and I don't want to take advantage of your soft heart, even though it would greatly benefit me to have all those quilts sold."*

"Don't worry, Beth," Solomon *had replied. "It will all work out."*

Beth seated herself at the kitchen table and went to work on another quilt. She deftly wielding her needle, mulling over different ways to save her farm. On the couch nearby, Peter slept. He was happily oblivious to their problems, and Beth was aware that that was how she always wanted it to be for him. She never wanted little Peter to ever feel any lack in his life.

All of a sudden, Beth realized that she was being selfish in holding on to the farm. She was doing it for herself, so that she would have some part of Ezekiel to hold on to.

She shook her head violently as she lay her work aside. But no, it wasn't selfish to think of handing over to Peter something that had belonged to his father and been important to him as well.

But Peter didn't remember Ezekiel, so what did it matter, she argued with herself. Of course, the fact that he didn't remember Ezekiel made it all the more important to ensure that Peter was left with a memory of his father in the form of the farm that had meant so much to him.

"I'm hungry *Mamm*," Peter announced suddenly. Beth realized that she had spent so much time sewing and pondering her problem, that it was supper time and she hadn't got Peter's meal ready.

"Oh, my little one," Beth murmured, jumping up and getting pots and pans on the stove.

"Who is it?" she called, as she heard a knock on the door.

"It's me, Rhoda," she heard a voice call back, and stopped short.

Ordinarily Beth would have been delighted to have Rhoda drop by, but now her friend's voice only reminded her that she needed to make a decision to sell her property and repay the people she owed money to.

"*Gut'n owed,*" Rhoda said, bustling into the room and picking Peter up as he ran over to her.

"*Gut'n owed*, Rhoda," Beth replied, trying to force some enthusiasm into her voice and finding herself unable to.

"I'm sorry, Beth," Rhoda said. "I don't mean to trouble you, but I just wanted to know if you've come to any decision about selling the farm. You see, there are people willing to buy your property, and I am here to help you find a place to stay."

"You're very kind, Rhoda," Beth replied. "And to answer your question, I have made a decision to sell the farm… and I have also found a buyer."

"Oh?" Rhoda said, looking surprised. "Who is it?"

"I'm not at liberty to reveal the name right now, but rest assured I will have the money soon, so that I can repay my debts and move on," Beth replied.

Rhoda heaved a sigh of relief. "That's good news for sure," she declared.

Beth nodded, thinking to herself how one person's good news was not such good news for another.

Chapter Four

Beth began to pace up and down again, stopping every little while to peer out of the window. Once or twice she walked out onto the porch and stood there until the cold drove her back inside again.

"*Mamm*, are you waiting for *Onkel* Sol?" Peter asked eagerly, running over to her. "I am too!"

"Oh no, dear, I'm not waiting for anybody," Beth replied hastily, silently asking the heavens for forgiveness for lying to her child.

"But you're walking up and down," Peter observed.

"To get some exercise, which I can't get outside because it's so cold," Beth responded with a laugh, scooping up the little boy.

The fact is, it had been three days since Solomon had come over and made his offer to buy her quilts and to ask after the farm. But now that she was ready to sell the farm, he hadn't visited as he had said he would. He also owed her money for the quilt he had taken, and Beth was beginning to worry that he had come to some harm, since it wasn't like him not to keep his word.

"Let's go for a buggy ride," Beth said to Peter.

Peter whooped in glee, and couldn't stay still as Beth wrapped a scarf around his neck and helped him into his jacket. It made little sense to leave the warmth of the fire and set off in the cold, but Beth was desperate. She needed to see Solomon without further delay and tell him of her decision to sell. And, she admitted, to make sure he was okay.

She shivered as she climbed into her buggy, and covered Peter with a blanket.

Her heart dropped a bit when she reached Solomon's house and stood outside knocking frantically. She realized he wasn't home, and probably hadn't been home for several days. Beth's heart plummeted, and she felt like the straw she had been clutching onto had suddenly given way and she was falling.

"Where's *Onkel* Sol?" Peter asked, pounding on the door with his tiny fists.

"He's not at home," Beth replied. "But don't worry, Peter, my darling. We're going to be just fine."

Beth rode over to Rhoda's house and knocked on her door.

"What is it Beth?" Rhoda asked, alarmed.

"I came here to ask if you could introduce me to the people who you said were interested in my farm."

"But I thought you'd found a buyer," Rhoda responded.

"I did. But he's missing, and I can't wait any longer," Beth answered.

Rhoda gave Beth a sympathetic look. "Of course," Rhoda said. "Right away."

"Come on Petey," Beth said, swinging her son into her arms. "We're going on another ride."

***

Beth sank into a sofa and lay back, watching her three-year-old son asleep beside her. This was no life for a little boy, being dragged from house to house like a peddler, asking people if they wanted to buy a farm.

"I'm sorry, Peter," Beth whispered, stroking his forehead as he slept. "We're going to be moving soon."

It had taken visits to several people in Hazel Grove Village before Beth found someone who actually had the money to buy her property. It had been a humbling experience, and Beth was grateful to Rhoda for taking over and doing most of the talking whenever she was too tired to make the sales pitch herself.

Beth fought the tears; thinking instead of happier winters with Ezekiel—the barrels of apples and pears, potatoes and beets. The harvest had always been so plentiful then. She got to her feet and went to the window, looking out at the fields, the stray tufts of green indicating where there were some stray beets and potatoes left to harvest.

With a determined sigh, she threw a cloak about her shoulders and went out to the barn to fetch some apples and pears from the rapidly depleting stock of fruit that lay there in crates. The person who was to buy her land was to come over the next day to begin the process. This was not like going to the market and selling a barrel of apples. These procedures took time, Rhoda had said. But the buyer had promised her an advance so that she could begin repaying her debts.

All at once, feeling the humiliation of her situation, Beth began to pray. Selling the farm that Ezekiel had worked so hard to maintain seemed wrong somehow, and Beth wasn't ready to give up the land. This seemed unfair, to first lose her husband and then her farm. And even a friend like Solomon, who had come into her life so suddenly and then disappeared almost as quickly. Why hadn't he even told her he was leaving Hazel Grove?

As she stood there in the barn, cradling a basket of apples and pears, her eyes strayed to the window. A solitary figure now stood in the field. Beth set the basket down and rushed out of the barn, hurrying towards the figure in the middle of the field.

"Who are you and what are you doing here?" Beth asked. The cloaked figure turned around and stared at Beth. It was a young woman, and she seemed both lost and scared.

"I'm sorry," she whispered.

"Are you alright?" Beth inquired gently. "Are you lost?"

The young woman was wearing Englischer clothes and seemed unfamiliar with the surroundings.

"I think I am lost," she said, trying to smile. "My father and I were here a few days ago, and I lost something. There was an accident with a man in a pony cart, and we got out to help. But I lost my bracelet, I think. So I got a ride back, and I was looking for it..."

"Pony cart? Do you mean buggy? Like we drive around here in our village?" Beth queried.

"Yes, that would be it. A buggy. With a man in it. He was injured. A car had run him off the road," the girl answered. "We stopped to help. I'm Penny Wayne, by the way."

"I'm Beth Fischer," Beth hastily introduced herself. "And I need to get back inside because I've left my baby son Peter by himself." She hesitated a little and then asked. "Do you know the name of the man who was hit?"

Penny nodded her head. "Yes, it is Solomon. My dad took him to the hospital in town, as he didn't appear to have any relatives here."

Beth's heart beat faster now.

"Do you know whether he was very badly injured?" Beth asked. "You see, I may very well know him. We all know each other in Hazel Grove Village."

"He said he was new here," Penny replied. "And he had injured his leg. My dad is visiting him right now, in fact. That's where I came from. I got a ride in a buggy, since we were so close. Do you think you could take me back to his house?"

With a quick nod, Beth picked Peter up and went to fetch the buggy.

"I've never been in one of these before," Penny said, climbing into the buggy, looking fascinated.

"It's a bumpy ride," Beth replied.

"I'm not afraid," Penny remarked. "In fact, I'm rather enjoying the adventure. I really enjoyed walking in your fields."

"I used to enjoy walking there as well, with my late husband, Ezekiel," Beth replied. "But everything's different now. I have to sell the property, because the farm isn't doing as well as it ought to."

"That's a pity," Penny said, "is there nothing you can do?"

Beth shook her head. "Regrettably, there's isn't much that I can do. I've done whatever I could and now I will sell the land and move."

"I'm sorry about your husband," Penny said.

"How old are you?" Beth asked.

"Fifteen," Penny replied.

"That's about the age I was when I met Ezekiel," Beth told her. "And we got married two years later."

"How old are you?" Penny asked curiously.

"Twenty-one," Beth replied. "By the way, what were you all doing out here, if you live out of the village?"

"We were coming here to meet one of dad's suppliers."

"Suppliers?" Beth queried.

"Yes," Penny nodded. "Dad is in the export business. He sources some wonderful things from this village. I'm going to join him after I graduate."

"We're here," Beth announced a minute later as they rounded a bend.

Beth climbed down from the buggy with Peter and went into Solomon's house. She paused in the doorway as she saw him hobbling about in a cast and using a cane to steady himself. There was a man there with him, who Beth guessed was Penny's father.

"Dad!" Penny called out, "I'm back! Were you worried?"

The man turned around and smiled at his daughter. "Well, I was, at first, when you disappeared. But Solomon assured me that the village was the safest place, and someone would bring you back eventually, in case you got lost."

"Well, here's my new friend, Beth Fischer. She was kind enough to bring me back in her buggy," Penny announced.

Solomon was staring at Beth in surprise. "Beth!" he greeted her.

"*Onkel* Sol! Peter cried, struggling out of Beth's arms and running to Solomon, who reached out to hug the little boy.

"Solomon, whatever happened to you?" Beth queried, entering the room hesitantly. "Petey, be careful...*Onkel* Sol is hurt."

"Beth," Penny said, drawing her attention away from Solomon. "This is my father, Robert Wayne."

"Robert rescued me," Solomon said, giving his rescuer a grateful smile.

"From what?" Beth asked, anxious. "We were all wondering where you had disappeared to."

"When I left your house after the last time we met, I was speeding along in my buggy when I was hit by a vehicle. I don't know what happened, but I was knocked out of my overturned buggy and fell by the wayside. It was a while later when Robert and Penny were driving by, that I managed to get to my feet, lean on the overturned buggy and wave them down. They were kind enough to stop for me... Robert drove me to the hospital, and I was there for a couple of days. I was a little out of it, and so did not get in touch with anyone to let them know. Then they took me back to their house to recover and brought me back early this morning. I was just going to find a way to contact you."

"And since there's nobody here to take care of Solomon," Robert said, "we are actually contemplating staying a couple of days."

"You've very kind," Beth breathed. "And Solomon, I'm so glad you're back safe. We had no idea where you were."

"I had no way of getting a message across to you," Solomon apologized.

Beth gave him a small smile. "It seems you're a little accident-prone."

"Why, has this sort of thing happened before?" Robert asked.

Solomon laughed. "Beth actually knocked me down with her buggy and that's how we met!"

"Oh my!" Penny exclaimed. "How did that happen?"

Beth gave her a self-deprecatory grin and shrugged. "I was lost in thought and drove my buggy off the road quite by accident. Solomon was taking a walk and unfortunately got knocked over."

"But unlike the vehicle that knocked my buggy over, Beth was kind enough to stop and then drive me back to her house, where she tended my not so serious wounds," Solomon added with a laugh.

"I was at Beth's house," Penny chimed in. "And I heard she is selling her farm and moving!"

"You are?" Solomon queried. "So you're accepting my offer?"

Beth looked away, wringing her hands in discomfort.

"What's going on, Beth?" Solomon asked.

"I wasn't going to sell, as you know," she replied. "But then I realized I had to. I just needed to do it, and have it done. So I came here to find you and tell you that you could buy the farm. But you weren't here, and I did not know where you were. So Ruby and I actually went from house to house looking for a buyer, and we finally found one."

"Oh, Beth!" Solomon exclaimed. "Are you comfortable selling?"

"Well, I didn't see any other way out," Beth murmured, keenly aware that Robert and Penny were listening to every word of this exchange.

"I told you I would buy your quilts," Solomon said. "I still stand by that offer."

"I couldn't let you do that, Solomon," Beth replied. "What would you do with so many?"

Solomon shrugged. "To be honest, I was going to buy them and then sell them for you.

They are exquisite, and I am absolutely certain they'd be gone in a flash."

Robert had been looking more and more interested in the conversation, and now interrupted.

"What is all this about quilts and farms? What's going on? Don't forget, I'm a businessman. Perhaps I can help," he said.

"Yes! My dad is awesome at buying and selling!" Penny declared.

"Beth is one of the most talented quiltmakers I know," Solomon explained. "She has made a fine collection…"

"It's my passion," Beth cut in. "I don't do it for commercial reasons."

"Which is what makes them so special," Solomon remarked.

"I'd like to see them," Robert said. "I have buyers who would be most interested if they are of the high standard of quality and uniqueness that Solomon has just described."

Beth looked uncertainly from Solomon to Robert. "You may see them," she replied.

"And Beth," Solomon said, hobbling over to her side, "please don't sell your property. I have another idea. I will lease it from you. The rent will help cover your… umm…"

"My debts?" Beth completed his sentence.

"Yes," Solomon said. "This is probably the best solution."

"But even as we speak, there's a buyer who is having papers drawn up to purchase the property," Beth said.

"Then we must explain that the deal is off," Solomon said. "I will pay you whatever price you name to lease the land."

"I leave that to you, Solomon," Beth replied.

"So you accept my offer?" Solomon asked.

"Yes, I do," Beth said, realizing she felt both grateful and relieved. "And I will go now and tell the prospective buyer that I have changed my mind."

"Solomon," Robert said, before Beth could leave, "would you and Beth be alright if we leave you for a little while and go take a look at Beth's quilts?"

"Yes, of course," Solomon said. "I am feeling a little tired, still, so I'll lie down for a while."

"I'll come back with some food," Beth called out to Solomon, as she followed Robert and Penny to their car.

"Vroom!" Peter said as the car started off. "Vroom…vroom!"

"This is his first time in a car," Beth laughed.

"Like it was my first time in a buggy," Penny chuckled.

Later, Robert leaned over the quilts that Beth lay before him. She stood back and breathlessly watched him pick up and inspect each one in detail.

"Remarkable," he murmured. "Quite remarkable."

"These quilts are beautiful!" Penny exclaimed, running her hands over the fabric and inspecting the patterns on each of them.

Robert straightened up and looked at Beth. "I want to buy all of them, and all the ones you make subsequently. I'll have some papers drawn up, but right now, if you would name your price…"

And so, Beth sold her first consignment of quilts and established herself as Robert's regular supplier of unique, exquisite handmade quilts, on the same day that Solomon told her he would lease her land so that she could stay on in her cottage. And just like that, the cloud that Beth had been under, was lifted.

"At last people in the village can look at me with something other than pitying eyes," Beth said to Rhoda a few days later. She had stopped by her house to hand over the money she owed her.

"They are now just filled with admiration at how you managed to get over your financial problems," Rhoda remarked.

"I have Solomon to thank… and Robert Wayne," Beth said. "You know what's so incredible?" she continued. "Solomon told me that he was on his way to town to meet someone who sourced handicrafts from our village. He wanted to find me a buyer for my quilts. And that's when he was knocked down by Robert and disappeared from Hazel Grove for all the time that we were desperately going around trying to find a buyer for my farm. And then, while talking to Robert, he got the idea about leasing my land instead of buying it so that I could stay on here."

She lifted Peter into her arms and climbed into her buggy. "I have to take some food across to Solomon's house," she added. "He has really been such a great help to me."

"You've been there a lot," Rhoda remarked, seeing Beth to the door. "And the village is beginning to buzz a little bit."

"After all the help Solomon has given me," Beth said, turning to hide her blush, "it's the least I can do."

Rhoda chuckled. "Yes, he even broke a leg for you!"

"Rhoda!" Beth said, aghast. "Don't talk like that!"

But as Beth drove away, she couldn't help feeling a small thrill of anticipation at the thought of seeing Solomon and spending some time chatting with him. He was full of plans for the farm and seemed so excited.

Chapter Five

"Your cast is off!" Beth exclaimed, as Solomon walked slowly up the porch steps. He steadied himself as Peter hurled himself into his arms.

"Peter, my son," Beth chided her child gently. "Be careful!"

"*Onkel* Sol, your leg is back!" Peter squealed.

Solomon laughed. "Indeed, it is Petey!" he replied, then turned to Beth.

"*Gute mariye,* Beth," he said, tipping his hat. "Busy with your quilting, I can see."

"Robert Wayne has placed another order. Apparently, my quilts are flying off the shelves," Beth answered happily.

"And they would too," Solomon replied. "They are truly exquisite."

Beth darted inside and returned to the porch carrying a quilt. "This is for you, Solomon," she said.

"It's not my birthday today, is it?" he laughed.

"This is to say thank you for buying the first quilt I ever sold, and then coming up with the best solution to my problem," she said. "I can now continue to look out across the fields from my bedroom window.”

“You didn’t have to do this,” Solomon said, with an almost bashful grin. “But I really love it and will treasure it.” He looked solemn. “I will work hard to turn things around at the farm, Beth,” he said, looking earnestly into her eyes.

Beth smiled. “I can’t wait for the harvest!”

“Hmmm, now I feel a lot of pressure to make sure the harvest meets your expectations!” Solomon joked with a twinkle in his eye. He looked down at Peter, who was still clinging to his hand. “Come on, little Peter, we’ve got work to do.”

“What could you possibly do in this weather?” Beth queried.

“Draw up plans for planting season, of course,” Solomon replied. “And clean out the barn.”

Beth smiled again. “Your energy is contagious,” she declared, taking a deep breath of the crisp winter air. “And so is your optimism. I feel hopeful. Very hopeful.”

As Solomon swung Peter up onto his shoulders and walked away towards the barn, Beth looked after them, becoming aware of an emotion that she thought she would never feel again. She blinked rapidly, willing the emotion away, and tore her eyes away from Solomon's broad, strong back and shoulders, on which her own dear son was so happily riding.

She delved into her pocket and took out the envelope in which Solomon had put the money he paid her for the quilt he had bought before his accident.

"To Beth," the note inside read, *"for knocking me down and then showing me that you can make the best friends in the most unusual circumstances. May this quilt be the first of the hundreds you go on to sell."*

"Best friends?" Beth queried to herself. "Could there be more to read between the lines?"

She shook the thought away. "This is ridiculous," she said aloud, turning back to her quilting and working her needle rapidly in and out of the fabric that fell across her knee. "I'm behaving like a young woman during courtship!"

She looked up from her work, and laying it aside, began to pace up and down the porch. It occurred to her that she was still a young woman, not so far past girlhood, except in terms of life experience.

"Oh, my!" Beth exclaimed, pacing more rapidly. "This can never be. I cannot, and will not, be disloyal to Ezekiel."

"You look deep in troubled thought," Rhoda observed. She had come up on the porch unnoticed, and Beth looked up, surprised. She had been deep in thought indeed, and worrying over her new feelings for Ezekiel.

"Oh dear, you've forgotten, haven't you?" Rhoda chucked. "You invited me over to lunch."

"Of course!" Beth said cheerily, jumping up, her mind rapidly putting together a menu.

"You forgot, didn't you?" Rhoda repeated. "Admit it, Beth," she said. "Admit that you forgot, because lately you've been so… distracted."

"I did forget, Rhoda," Beth replied. "Only because I've been so busy with my quilts. The orders are coming in faster than I can sew."

Rhoda laughed. "I was teasing you. You didn't invite me to lunch. I was passing by and decided to drop in on you, that's all. And about your quilt orders, maybe you need to put together a team of seamstresses. You design the quilts, and they can do the work while you keep a close eye on quality."

"Why didn't I think of that?" Beth queried, looking at Rhoda in astonishment.

"Because, like I said earlier, you've been distracted," she declared. As she spoke, she cocked an eye at Solomon's buggy, parked in the driveway.

Beth blushed and shook her head violently. "No! No! That's not true at all! I am very loyal to Ezekiel!"

"Oh, Beth," Rhoda said with a gentle sigh, "you will always be loyal to Ezekiel. You can never forget him. He is Petey's *daed*. But you're so young. And Peter needs a father. Boys do, you know. Besides, Ezekiel wouldn't want you to go forward without someone by your side."

She took Beth's hand. "Beth, my dear, I do believe Ezekiel set his whole thing up, from up there in heaven."

Beth stared at Rhoda, horrified, and sank into a chair, drawing her shawl protectively about her shoulders. "I forgive you for imagining things, Rhoda," she replied, "because no doubt you do so out of concern for me. But I want to assure you, I can look out for myself. I am quite independent now, and Peter is happy. He can play with Solomon whenever he wants."

"True," Rhoda replied with a shrug. "And what about when Peter is older and needs to be shown his way around the farm, and how to navigate life itself?" she asked.

"I think I can teach my son quite well, Rhoda," Beth answered firmly.

"Of course you think you can, Beth, and maybe you even will. But I think Peter deserves to have two parents to raise him. The good Lord above planned it that way. A truly balanced family is one where there are two parents, like the two pans of a weighing scale."

"Everything alright?" Solomon asked, coming up the steps with Peter still on his shoulders.

"Yes, of course," Beth replied, her cheeks turning pink. "Why would it be otherwise?"

"I guess I should be off," Rhoda declared.

"Why don't you stay to lunch, Rhoda? I'll whip something up," Beth said hurriedly, not welcoming the prospect of spending time alone in Solomon's company.

"Sure, I'd love to," Rhoda replied. "And I'm sure Solomon would like to as well."

"Unless he has things to do at home, which I'm sure he does, right Solomon?" Beth replied, looking from Rhoda to Solomon.

"*Onkel* Sol, eat lunch with me!" Peter said, and Beth sighed. Solomon couldn't refuse Peter anything, not even a request to give him a piggyback ride when his leg was fresh out of his cast.

"Well, I'll go fix lunch, then," Beth said, trying hard not to notice Solomon's curly dark hair when he took off his hat, and his deep blue eyes when he looked into hers. She caught her breath in her throat and turned to hide the redness in her cheeks.

"I'm quite a good cook, you know," Solomon announced. He had followed her into the kitchen, offering to help. "Because I've been living on my own so much."

"I see," Beth said breathlessly, amidst a clatter of pots and pans.

"What I'm saying is, let me help. You don't need to do everything on your own, you know, Beth," Solomon said, his voice firm but gentle.

"Thank you, Solomon," Beth answered, taking a pie out of the oven. She was unwilling to allow herself to hear the message between the words that Solomon had just spoken.

"You couldn't have made that just now," Rhoda remarked, indicating the pie as she stepped into the kitchen just behind Solomon.

"Well, I made it early this morning, actually. I enjoy baking, and it calms me to have the smell of sweet apples and pie crust," Beth replied.

Within seconds there was laughter in the kitchen, and a warm blanket of comfort and joy settled over them as they sat at the table eating apple pie, cold meat, bread and cheese.

"So, Solomon," Rhoda began, "I suggested to Beth that since she is getting so many orders for her quilts, so many that she can barely keep up with them, she should think of setting up a workshop and hiring seamstresses to do all the work while she supervises."

"Wouldn't that affect the quality and uniqueness?" Beth queried.

"Actually, I think that is a splendid idea, Rhoda," Solomon said.

"But where would this workshop be?" Beth asked. "There isn't enough space in the cottage."

"We could build you one by the barn," Solomon said enthusiastically, "so that you can look out at the fields that you love, and have enough space for your team of seamstresses… plus space to store the quilts."

"That certainly sounds like a great idea," Rhoda enthused, but Beth was silent.

"I wouldn't know where to begin," she said eventually.

"You need a man for the job," Solomon declared. "And here's one who is willing and able."

"Surely you can't build a workshop all by yourself?" Beth remarked.

"No, not at all," Solomon said with a broad smile. "We'll organize a *frolic*… and you can leave that to me."

***

Later, out on the porch, Rhoda waited only until Solomon's buggy had rolled out of the gate. Then she turned to Beth with shining eyes.

"Beth, he is definitely interested in you," she whispered. "Actually, more than interested, judging by the way he looks at you."

"Solomon is becoming a very good friend and he really loves Peter," Beth said hastily. "Besides, I am still devoted to Ezekiel."

"And so you always will be, my dear," Rhoda said. "But you need happiness, and I am certain that Ezekiel would never want you to be lonely."

"Well, perhaps," Beth said, then changed the subject. "Where do I begin finding a team of seamstresses?" she asked looking worried. "Now that Solomon's going to be organizing a *frolic*, I need to get my seamstresses together."

"I have a few people that I could recommend," Rhoda said.

"You've been a good friend," Beth replied. "Thank you, Rhoda."

"If you really think of me as a friend, Beth," Rhoda said solemnly, "please do give Solomon a thought. Pay attention to the signs that he is interested."

She left before Beth could respond, and Beth took Peter's hand and led him indoors.

Chapter Six

Beth ran out onto the porch when she heard Peter squeal.

"Petey! What's wrong?" she burst out and then stopped. "Solomon, *gute mariye*! You're here early!"

"There's snow expected tomorrow, so we've called everyone to finish building your workshop today," Solomon replied, rubbing his hands together.

"Oh!" Beth exclaimed. "In that case I'll get breakfast ready for everyone to eat."

"You don't have to go to all that trouble," Solomon reassured her.

"I have been up early… baking," Beth said. "So there's fresh bread, bacon and eggs, and pancakes with my homemade blueberry preserve."

"If you give us such a feast, we might not be inclined to get any work done at all," Solomon laughed.

"And there's hot cocoa for you too," Beth added with a smile.

"Thank you, Beth," Solomon said, taking the mug of steaming hot cocoa from her and sitting by the fire to wait for the men of Hazel Grove village to gather for the frolic.

"I have now got a team of seven seamstresses," Beth said. She felt her voice shake just a bit, and she tried to calm herself. She could feel Solomon's eyes on her, and it made her heart race.

"All the more reason why we need to get the workshop finished," Solomon declared.

"*Onkel* Sol, can you play ball with me?" Peter asked, and Beth heaved a silent sigh of relief.

"Yes of course, little man," Solomon said, jumping up immediately and swinging Peter up into his arms. Beth could feel her heart swell with overwhelming joy as she watched them play outside, and Rhoda's words echoed in her mind. Peter needed a father. Even as the thought came to her mind, she felt peace.

"You look… different," Solomon remarked, when he came back inside with Peter.

Beth gave him a quizzical look. She was dressed as she always was, in a dark blue gown and white *kaap*.

"In what way?" she queried.

"Well, I can't say exactly," Solomon replied. "But I just felt this warmth and peace when I walked back inside… and you were glowing."

Beth didn't say anything but looked at Solomon in silence.

"Beth," he began. "I don't know how to put this, but…"

"Oh, there come the others," Beth said quickly, hurrying to look out of the window, and shattering the moment.

***

"Why did you cut him off when he was going to say something profound?" Rhoda chided Beth later, as they got busy preparing lunch for the men who were still hard at work.

"We don't know that it was going to be profound, as you put it," Beth replied.

"Well, I'm not going to say anything more, except, let Solomon have his say. The good Lord knows it's the right thing to do." Rhoda said firmly.

"We're serving the food in the barn," Beth announced, as the womenfolk of Hazel Grove arrived with trays of pies and casseroles, and pots of stew.

Moments later she was standing in the barn, looking around her in awe.

"What are these for?" she asked, as Solomon approached her with a huge smile.

"These?" Solomon queried, indicating the three large closets that dwarfed the trestle tables laid out for the food in the middle of the barn.

"They're for the most lovely quilts ever made," Solomon replied. "I figured you would need them for storage, since you now have a team making the quilts and are looking at expanding your business."

"Oh, Solomon," Beth said, overcome. "You are really most kind. You have done so much for me already, and now this…"

"Well," Solomon said, in a voice meant only for her ears, "I told you – you don't have to do everything yourself. You have me, Beth. And I would like to be there for you." He paused to take a breath. "And not just as a friend, but…"

"Solomon!" someone called, and the moment was interrupted yet again. Only this time Beth wasn't relieved. She wanted to hear what he had been trying to tell her for a while.

"What did he say?" Rhoda asked, as they began to serve the men.

"He didn't get to completing his sentence," Beth replied. "And I didn't get to thank him for making me the most beautiful closets… without me suspecting a thing."

"Like I said before, I do believe Ezekiel set this up from above, Beth," Rhoda replied. "And Solomon seems like someone who will take good care of you." She giggled. "Not to mention that he is also very handsome," she finished with a flourish.

Beth blushed and glanced over at Solomon. He was sitting at a table with his hat off, his thick mop of dark hair falling over his brow. As she looked in his direction, Solomon looked up, and their eyes met for a brief moment.

Beth escaped from the barn and walked rapidly towards the cottage, eager to run up to her room and think over this new turn of events.

"*Mamm*!" she heard a tiny voice call, and turned around to see Peter running after her.

"Can we go for a walk with *Onkel* Sol?" Peter asked.

"When, my child?" Beth asked, taking Peter's hand and turning back towards the cottage.

"Tomorrow?" a voice said, and Beth turned around again, her breath catching in her throat.

"Yes," she said, finding her smile. "I would like that very much."

***

"I am happy to be up and about again," Solomon declared as they set off the next day. "Having my leg in a cast was hard…" He turned to Beth and smiled at her. "But having you there every day, bringing me food that you had cooked, and tidying up for me… that more than made up for missing out on my walks."

"It was the least I could do," Beth replied, the blood rushing to her cheeks.

"That period of time, confined to my house, also made me realize how grateful I am to the good Lord above for bringing you my way when I was out walking that fateful day."

"To knock you over?" Beth laughed, her shyness suddenly leaving her.

"Well," Solomon said, "I'll tell you a secret. You didn't just knock me over… you stole my heart."

"Oh!" Beth exclaimed, bashful again. Solomon had stopped in the exact spot where that first accident had occurred, and was looking at her with an expression in his eyes that set her heart racing. Peter, whose hand Solomon was holding, was looking up at her too.

"Beth," Solomon said, "I realize that it's time I stopped walking alone. For me now, the long walk ahead would only have meaning, if you would walk with me."

"I… don't… understand," Beth murmured.

"Walk with me, Beth. Every day." His face grew more serious. "For the rest of our lives. Would you Beth? Would you consider letting me into your life and into your heart?"

Beth was tongue-tied.

"*Mamm*," Peter piped up. "Can *Onkel* Sol be my *Daed*?"

Beth's eyes widened in surprise and Solomon looked at Peter with a grin.

"Peter just took the words out of my mouth," Solomon said, gazing into Beth's eyes with an intensity that made her almost dizzy. "Would you marry me, Beth?"

Chapter Seven

"And you said yes?" Rhoda squealed.

"Except it seemed odd that he asked to marry me rather than court me," Beth remarked.

"Oh Beth, don't you see? He's been courting you for months now without you even realizing it. That trip he attempted to make, to find you a buyer for your quilts; organizing the frolic so you would have a workshop… and even making you those incredible closets with his own hands," Rhoda said. "And of course, his love for Peter was so apparent."

"I can't believe my good fortune," Beth said, her hand on her heart.

"You deserve happiness, Beth," Rhoda said. "And Peter will have a wonderful *Daed*."

Beth smiled to herself. Her life had changed. Her world came together, the void was filled… and winter didn't seem so cold after all.

And from somewhere up in Heaven, she imagined Ezekiel smiling down at her, content and happy now that she was finally at peace.

The End

FREE GIFT

Just to say thanks for checking our works we like to gift you

Our Exclusive Never Before Released Books

100% FREE!

Please GO TO

http://cleanromancepublishing.com/gift

And get your FREE gift

Thanks for being such a wonderful client.

Please Check out My Other Works

By checking out the link below

http://cleanromancepublishing.com/rbauth

Thank You

Many thanks for taking the time to buy and read through this book.

It means lots to be supported by SPECIAL **readers like** YOU**.**

Hope you enjoyed the book; please support my writing by leaving an honest review to assist other readers.

With Regards,

Ruth Bawell

www.ingramcontent.com/pod-product-compliance
Lightning Source LLC
Chambersburg PA
CBHW031133160726

47989CB00017B/2911